Snap *books*™

Cheerleading

Cheers, Chants, and Signs

Getting the Crowd Going

by Jen Jones

Content Consultant

Kristalynn Russell

Director and Choreographer,
Colorado Rapids Cheerleaders
Commerce City, Colorado

Capstone *press*®

Mankato, Minnesota

Snap Books are published by Capstone Press,
151 Good Counsel Drive, P.O. Box 669, Mankato, Minnesota 56002.
www.capstonepress.com

Printed in the United States of America in North Mankato, Minnesota.
082009
005600R

Library of Congress Cataloging-in-Publication Data
Jones, Jen.
      Cheers, chants, and signs: Getting the crowd going / by Jen Jones.
      p. cm. — (Snap books. Cheerleading)
      Summary: "Upbeat text reveals how to make, practice, and execute cheers, chants,
and signs and provides many examples of each" — Provided by publisher.
Includes bibliographical references and index.
      ISBN-13: 978-1-4296-1347-7 (hardcover)
      ISBN-10: 1-4296-1347-5 (hardcover)
      1. Cheers — Juvenile literature. 2. Cheerleading — Juvenile literature.
I. Title. II. Series.
LB3635.J625 2008
791.6'4 — dc22   200718167

Editorial Credits

Jenny Marks, editor; Kim Brown, designer; Jo Miller, photo researcher

Photo Credits

Table of Contents

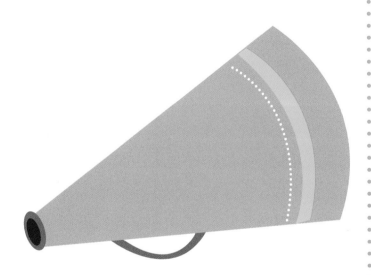

INTRODUCTION

Sizzling Spirit

Today's cheerleaders have a crowd-thrilling reputation. What crowd isn't wowed by dazzling tumbling and daring stunts? Yet it's important to never lose sight of the sport's purpose. Cheerleading is just that — leading cheers! More than 100 years after the sport began, the heart of cheer remains the same.

In this book, you'll learn to stir up spirit by using the basics — cheers, chants, and signs. These key cheer tools can fire up the crowd and inspire the team. Being on the sidelines has never been so much fun.

Chapter 1

GIMME A C-H-E-E-R

Put the "C" in Cheerleading

To the untrained eye, cheers and chants may appear to be the same. To a cheerleader, that's like saying there's no difference between high heels and high-tops! Sure, they're both types of shoes. But you'd never wear heels to gym class. It's the same with chants and cheers.

Chants are short, catchy phrases that are repeated several times. Squads use chants to rally the team during tense game moments or to pep up the crowd.

Cheers are longer in length than chants. While chants have very simple moves, cheers use more impressive motions, jumps, and stunts.

Jazz It Up

Years ago, cheers were pretty simple. They featured big megaphones, basic motions, and the occasional jump for joy. Today's cheer routines require more strength and skill. Fancy choreography is now the norm. Keep your cheers fun and flashy with these tips.

Use formations to create funky visual effects for the crowd. Diamonds, "Vs," and staggered lines are all popular formations. Tumble, dance, or jog from one formation to the next.

Sprinkle some sass into routines with sparkly poms. Use them to form letters, or create a sizzling ripple effect with a peel-off. For added drama, try shaking them during free throws and field goals.

Stunting and tumbling add the "wow" factor to your cheers. Grab the crowd's attention with awe-inspiring pyramids, mounts, basket tosses, and gymnastics.

Spread the Spirit

Have you ever seen "the wave" make the rounds at a sporting event? It's a domino effect of fan support. There is no doubt that spirit is contagious. As a cheerleader, you start the first ripples of excitement. If fans sense your high energy, they're likely to get revved up too.

Cheers, chants, and signs are awesome ways to shift a crowd's spirit into high gear. Check out these ideas for escalating energy.

Keep the cheers coming. Goofing around has no place on the sidelines. Your squad's captain should call cheers or chants every few minutes to keep the spirit flowing.

Find strength in numbers. Create a special cheering section where super fans unite. Pass out face paint, pom-poms, and other special treats. Only the loudest and proudest get these special seats.

Cheer even when not cheering. Between cheers, pump up the crowd with wiggling spirit fingers, small stunts, or high kicks. Make sure to yell encouragement like, "Come on, defense!" or "Let's go, Wildcats!"

Leading Ladies

As a cheerleader, all eyes are on you. Do you know how to keep the crowd's attention? Showmanship is the name of the game. Don't just go through the motions. Sell what you yell! Want to make sure your performance packs punch? Check out these tips!

Put on your happy face. No one wants to see a sour or bored cheerleader. A big smile goes the extra mile.

Stay sharp. While cheering or chanting, make sure your motions are crisp and defined. Try to hit them without overextending.

Pump up the volume. Project your voice loud and clear to the crowd. (Remember, no sing-song voices. This isn't choir practice!)

Make eye contact. Keep your head up and be confident. Eye contact helps you connect with the crowd.

Good Sports

Cheer opportunities span the sports world. Of course, most squads can't cheer for every team at school. When you're not on the sidelines, show your spirit by attending games as a fan. Teams without official cheer squads will really appreciate the support. To get you started, try these cheers and chants for almost any sport.

14

"X" = pause or clasp

Generic Cheers

Cats X let's hear you yell
"We want a win!"
(We want a win!)
Cats X let's hear you spell
"B-H-S"
(B-H-S)
BHS XX let's win!

Generic Chants

Fire up X Cats
Fire up! XX

When we say "go,"
you say "fight!"
Go (Fight!)
Go (Fight!)
When we say "win,"
you say "tonight!"
Win (Tonight!)
Win (Tonight!)
Put it all together, Cats
Go, fight, win, tonight!

All you Wildcats in the house
Let's cheer
Ooh, it's getting hot in here!

Gridiron Glory

Fall is in the air, fans are filling the stadiums, and homecoming is just around the corner. It must be football season! This time of year is bursting with excitement. And of course, cheerleaders are at the heart of it all. Score big with these football cheer tips.

Dress the part. Short skirts aren't much fun in freezing temperatures. Accessorize with cute scarves, leggings, or earmuffs — in school colors, of course.

Make it fun. Launch T-shirts and mini-footballs into the stands. Do push-ups or high kicks for every touchdown. These traditions will make your squad unforgettable.

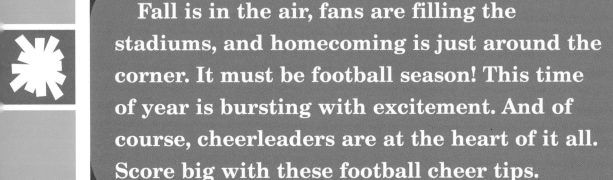

Football Cheers

Touchdown X Wildcats X
Don't give in
Touchdown X Wildcats X
We want a win!

Get up on your feet X
And yell really loud
Come on X get up XX
Wildcat crowd!

Football Chants

Sack X that X quarterback
Cats XX attack

S-C-O-R-E
Score X seven more

Push 'em back
Push 'em back
Go Big D!

Hot Shots

Game-winning free throws. Amazing three-pointers. Players speeding up and down the court. Basketball season is full of fast-paced fun! And cheerleaders see it all from their prime spot on the sidelines. Follow these tips to get nothing but net.

Take the floor. Halftime and quarter breaks are great times to show your stuff on the court. Short dance routines and chants are sure to keep the crowd pumped as the team recharges.

Keep the energy up. There are few places where spirit runs higher than in a basketball arena. Noise levels skyrocket, fans go crazy, and the team feeds off the energy. It's your job to keep it that way. Encourage the crowd to yell along with you.

Basketball Cheers

Take it to the top, big blue
Push it to the limit X
The [school name] team is really hot
Wildcats gonna win it!

The blue and gray are back X
And better than before X
Get ready for the Wildcat heat
As we take the floor!

Basketball Chants

Dribble it X
Just a little bit XX

Take that ball away
Defense, take that ball away!

Hit that shot, Cats
We want a basket

Wildcats X get tough X
Show 'em X your stuff! XX

Let the Beat Hit 'em

From the band to the mascot to the color guard, many schools have a full-on spirit patrol. By joining forces, you can put on one seriously awesome show. Use these ideas for setting the stage at games and pep rallies.

Most squads dance along with the school fight song. It can be fun to prepare some additional routines too. Snag the pep band's playlist for the season to see what it has in store. Choose three or four songs and brainstorm fun routines. Be sure to incorporate dance, chants, and stunts.

Make friends with the school mascot. Mascots definitely know how to rile up the crowd. Ask that crazy creature to join your squad in chants. Better yet, put your mascot on top of a stunt.

In It to Win It

Spirit-raising doesn't stop at sporting events. Many cheer squads transport the sideline fun to cheer competitions. Winning routines rely on more than just skill. Presentation is key! Rev up the crowd with eye-catching signs and easy-to-follow cheers. Impress the judges and competing teams with these winning tips.

Make it easy for the crowd. Don't just tell the crowd what to say. Show them! Accent your words with stunts and motions. If you want the crowd to yell "blue and gray," throw one stunt up on each word. Want even better crowd participation? Have each flier hold a sign at the top.

Feel the flow. Rushing through your cheers confuses the crowd and lowers your score. Yell each word loudly and clearly. Cheers with a simple, steady pace let the fans chime in.

Competition Cheer

Cats X
Let's hear you shout
Yell with us
And spell it out
C-A-T-S
Cats get tough
(C-A-T-S)
(Cats get tough!)

Competition Chants

Yell for the best X
B-H-S

Hey blue XX
Hey gray
Let's go XX all the way!

Wildcats, get to it X
BHS Let's do it!

Signs that Shine

Every squad has its bag of tricks. Cheerleaders sport fun props like megaphones, pom-poms, and spirit sticks. But what spirit-leading tool is the most effective? Signs! Seeing the words makes it a breeze for crowds to cheer along. Want to speak proper "sign language"? Follow these tips for signs that are oh so fine.

Go big and bold. Don't clutter your signs with long phrases. Your crowd will be stuck squinting. Each sign should display just one letter or word in large, thick print.

Avoid an "oops" moment. When prepping signs before a cheer, make sure they aren't in the wrong order or upside down. An arrow on the back works wonders.

Think outside the box. When making signs, paperboard is a reliable standby. But it's fun to experiment with creative materials. Some squads use boxes to make lettered blocks. Others show off in spandex bodysuits with letters or words. Whether you're wearing the sign or holding it, make sure to work it.

I Saw the Sign

Peanut butter and jelly. Mary-Kate and Ashley. Hammer and nails. Signs and cheers. No doubt about it, signs and cheers fit perfectly together. But signs can be used in so many other ways.

A "run-through" banner is a high-energy way to kick off a game. As the team is announced, the players tear through the banner and run onto the field. Most banners display giant mascot drawings or win-worthy phrases like, "Sink the Seahawks!"

Who says spirit has to be saved for games? Start the party early by plastering your school with signs. Gather up tons of markers, glitter, paper, and paint, and let your creative juices flow. Try simple but classic phrases like "Wildcats are #1" or "BHS is the Best." With your school's permission, deck out hallways, lockers, and the gym.

Inspire the Crowd

You've learned how to fire up the crowd with cheers and chants. Plus, you can whip up dazzling signs like a pro. Why not put your new skills into practice? Energize your next big game with these sign-friendly cheers and chants.

For this cheer, make signs spelling out "Victory"

Wildcat X victory
Spell it out on the count of three
1, 2, 3, hit it!
V-I-C-T-O-R-Y
Once more
V-I-C-T-O-R-Y!

For this cheer, make signs reading "Go," "Big," and "[school color]"

Cats on the left yell "go"
(Go!)
Cats in the middle yell "big"
(Big!)
Cats on the right yell "blue"
(Blue!)
Yell it all together, Cats
(Go Big Blue!)

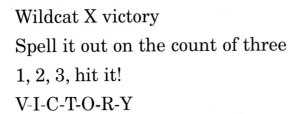

For this chant, make signs spelling your school's initials

Simply X the best
Better than the rest X
Who are we yelling for?
B-H-S!

One thing all cheerleaders are good at is being proud of their teams. Their cheers, chants, and signs are major confidence-boosters for the team. Win or lose, players and fans appreciate a cheerleader's energy and support. So stay postive. And, no matter how the game is going, show that winning spirit!

GLOSSARY

defense (DEE-fenss) — a sports team trying to prevent the other team from scoring

formation (for-MAY-shuhn) — the positions in which cheerleaders stand to make a visual shape

flier (FLY-ur) — a person on top of a mount

peel-off (PEEL-AWF) — choreography in which all cheerleaders do the same move at different times, creating a rippling visual effect

showmanship (SHOH-min-ship) — the ability to entertain and perform

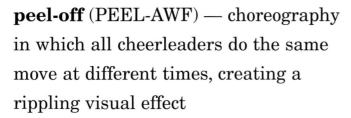

FAST FACTS

Cheerleading got its start at the University of Minnesota thanks to a catchy chant from student Johnny Campbell. Campbell got crowds chanting the now famous chant, "Rah, rah, rah! Ski-U-Mah! Varsity, varsity, Minnesota!"

In the United States, at least 4 million girls and women participate in cheerleading from the junior high school to college level.

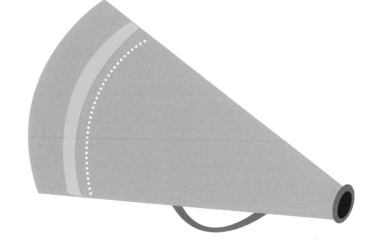

READ MORE

Carrier, Justin, and Donna McKay. *Complete Cheerleading.* Champaign, Ill.: Human Kinetics, 2006.

Jones, Jen. *Cheer Basics: Rules to Cheer By.* Cheerleading. Mankato, Minn.: Capstone Press, 2006.

Singer, Lynn. *Cheerleading.* New York: Rosen, 2007.

INTERNET SITES

FactHound offers a safe, fun way to find Internet sites related to this book. All of the sites on FactHound have been researched by our staff.

Here's how

1. Visit *www.facthound.com*

2. Choose your grade level.

3. Type in this book ID **1429613475** for age-appropriate sites. You may also browse subjects by clicking on letters, or by clicking on pictures and words.

4. Click on the **Fetch It** button.

FactHound will fetch the best sites for you!

ABOUT THE AUTHOR

While growing up in Ohio, Jen Jones spent seven years as a cheerleader for her grade school and high school squads. (Not surprisingly, she was voted "Most Spirited" several times by her classmates.) Following high school, she became a coach and spurred several cheer teams to competition victory. For two years, she cheered and choreographed on the cheer squad for the Chicago Lawmen, a semi-professional football team.

As well as teaching occasional dance and cheer workshops, Jen now works in sunny Los Angeles as a freelance writer for publications like *American Cheerleader, Cheer Biz News,* and *Dance Spirit.* She is also a member of the Society of Children's Book Writers and Illustrators.

Index